GETTING READY FOR
FIRST GRADE

Written by **Vera Ahiyya, The Tutu Teacher**
Illustrated by **Debby Rahmalia**

A Random House PICTUREBACK® Book

Random House 🏠 New York

It's the first day of school. Nana, Noa, and I sit at the kitchen table and eat loco moco.

"Are you ready for first grade, Leilani?" Noa asks.

"I think so," I say with a shrug.

"Are you a bit worried?" Nana asks.

"Well," I sigh, "I already know how to do school, but I don't know how to do *first grade*."

"It's okay to be nervous, Leilani," she replies. "First grade is full of exciting new firsts! You just have to be open to trying new things."

Noa and I put on our new shoes and backpacks.
We race to the car and buckle ourselves in.
When we get to school, we take a picture together.
"Cheese!" Noa and I say.

Inside the classroom, my new teacher greets me with a big smile.
"Hi, Leilani!" Mr. White says. "Welcome to first grade!"

I look around the room and see some kids from
kindergarten! I smile and wave at my friend Saraiya.
Mr. White shows me to my cubby and helps me unpack.

"Please find a spot in the circle," Mr. White says. "Then we will all go around and say our name and favorite color."

When it's my turn, I say, "I'm Leilani, and my favorite color is purple!"

Some of the other students sign, "Me too." This makes me feel good.

Next, Mr. White shows us our daily schedule. We will have math, science, word building, reading, and "specials." That means each day, we go to a special class like Physical Education, Library, Art, or Music.

Daily Schedule
- Math
- Science
- Word Building
- Reading

- ★ Specials ★
- Phys. Ed.
- Library
- Art
- Music

Mr. White then gives a tour of the classroom. There are so many fun "centers," like a bookcase full of books, a math space to practice counting and addition, and a makerspace where we can create and build new ideas.

Wow, first grade is going to be great!

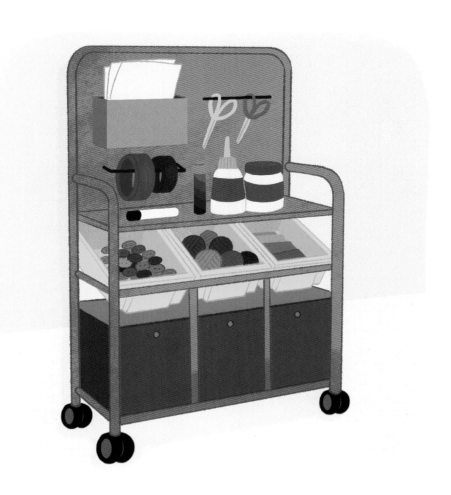

"Next, I have a special treat—journals!" Mr. White says. "They're just for you, and you can write and draw anything you'd like in them."

My very own journal! I wonder what I'll put in there.

Soon, it's time to line up for lunch. I'm really excited. This year, I get to go through the cafeteria line all by myself! A sign at the front shows what's on today's menu: pizza or a hamburger.

"Pizza, please!" I say when it's my turn to choose.

I add a couple more things to my tray, then carry it over to a table where Saraiya is sitting. She is talking to a girl from our class I don't know. At first, I feel a little left out, but when they see me, they both make room so I can sit with them. Whew!

"Hi, my name is Hannah!" the other girl says. "This is my new school!"

"I'm Leilani," I tell her. "Do you like it here so far?"

"I LOVE it!" Hannah shouts. "But there is a lot to learn."

Wow. I was worried about starting a new grade, and Hannah is starting at a whole new school!

During recess, we play tag, and Hannah runs so fast I can barely keep up. Before we know it, more kids join in. Soon, the whole grade is playing tag!

Phweet!

The whistle sound means it's time to line up. Hannah doesn't know our recess rules yet, so I show her to our class line. Helping my new friend really makes me feel ready for first grade!

Once we're back in the classroom, Mr. White tells us we can now find a partner and explore our room centers.

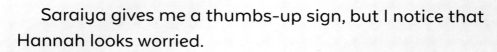

Saraiya gives me a thumbs-up sign, but I notice that Hannah looks worried.

"Are you okay?" I ask her.

"I don't have a partner," she replies.

"Don't worry," I say. "Mr. White, can Saraiya, Hannah, and I work together?"

"Of course, Leilani," Mr. White says. "That's a wonderful idea."

We head over to the reading center and each pick out a book.

"Thanks for helping me," Hannah whispers.

"You're welcome," I whisper back. "I'm happy to help!"

A timer goes off, and we move on to the math center. Mr. White has put out a basket of math cubes. We count together all the way to one hundred!

"We're almost out of cubes!" Saraiya laughs.

Before we know it, the timer goes off again.

"You may now have free-choice time by yourselves," Mr. White tells us.

Hannah goes back to the reading center to finish her book. Saraiya goes to the carpet to practice yoga. I bring my new journal to the makerspace.

I grab a crayon and open the journal. I draw a picture of my day and add lots of purple. I can't wait to show Noa and Nana!

I put my journal in my backpack just in time for closing circle.

GLUE

"First graders," Mr. White says, "let's make a list of all your amazing firsts today."

"Today I went to a new school!" Hannah announces.

"I tried a new yoga pose!" Saraiya says, beaming.

"I drew a picture of my first day!" I share proudly.

It is now time to go home. We line up and walk to the dismissal area. I wave goodbye to my friends. I can't believe our first day is already over!

Soon, I see Nana and Noa! They give me a big hug.

"How was your first day?" Nana asks.

"It was great!" I say, showing her my journal.

"You were right. I'm all ready for first grade!"

VERA AHIYYA, The Tutu Teacher, was raised in El Paso, Texas, by her wonderful mother and amazing grandparents. Vera has been an early childhood educator for over fifteen years. Her online presence is dedicated to influencing other educators by spreading her vast knowledge and love of inclusive children's books. She is the author of *Rebellious Read Alouds,* a professional development book for educators. In addition to the Getting Ready series, she is the author of three other picture books: *You Have a Voice, KINDergarten,* and *Look How Much I've Grown in KINDergarten.*

DEBBY RAHMALIA is an illustrator and storyteller based in Indonesia. She graduated from Bandung Institute of Technology, where she earned a Bachelor of Interior Design degree. Debby's long-term dream was to become an illustrator. She was encouraged to pursue her dream after she had her first baby and has been illustrating ever since. One of her dreams is to share the books she illustrates with her child and to enjoy them together.